MARISABINA RUSSO

A Visit to Oma

Greenwillow Books, New York

For my mother, Sabina,
and
Tante Anny
and
Tante Emmy

Gouache paints were used for the full-color art.
The text type is Windsor Old Style Light.

Printed in Hong Kong by
South China Printing Company (1988) Ltd.
First Edition   10 9 8 7 6 5 4 3 2 1

Library of Congress Cataloging-in-Publication Data

Russo, Marisabina.
A visit to Oma / by Marisabina Russo.
p.   cm.
Summary: When a child visits her great-grandmother
who speaks to her in an unfamiliar language,
she makes up a story in her own head to fit her
great-grandmother's gestures.
ISBN 0-688-09623-9   ISBN 0-688-09624-7 (lib. bdg.)
[1. Great-grandmothers—Fiction.]   I. Title.
PZ7.R9192Vi   1991
[E]—dc20   89-77716   CIP   AC

My great-grandmother lives with my aunt
and uncle in their apartment. She has her
own room at the end of the hall.
On Sundays we always visit them.

The first thing my mother says when we come to the door is, "Celeste, go see your Oma." Oma is what we call my great-grandmother.
I walk down the long hall and knock on Oma's door.

"Come," she calls.

I open the door slowly, and there she is, waiting for me. She always wears the same dress. It is black with deep pockets. "Come, come," says Oma. I think that "come" is the only word she knows in English.

It is always dark in Oma's room. She likes to keep the curtains drawn. The only light is in the ceiling. A long string hangs from it, to turn it on and off. It is just the right length for Oma and me to reach. We are the same size.

First Oma hugs me. She always smells like oranges. Then she strokes my face and smiles. Oma's smile is sad.
Oma points to a chair, and I sit down. She offers me candy that looks like a slice of fruit. It is red and coated with sugar. I nibble it to make it last longer.

Then Oma sits in a chair facing me and starts to talk in a language I don't understand. Oma smiles, she frowns, she looks surprised, she almost cries, and all the while her hands wave shapes in the air. I just nod and sit there.

But while Oma talks, I make up my own story
to go with what her face and hands seem to say.
Today my story goes like this:

When Oma was a young girl, her mother and father decided whom she would marry.
He was the son of a wealthy merchant. His name was Morris.

There was one problem. Oma didn't like Morris. He was lazy, vain, and boring. But she had to marry him, anyhow.

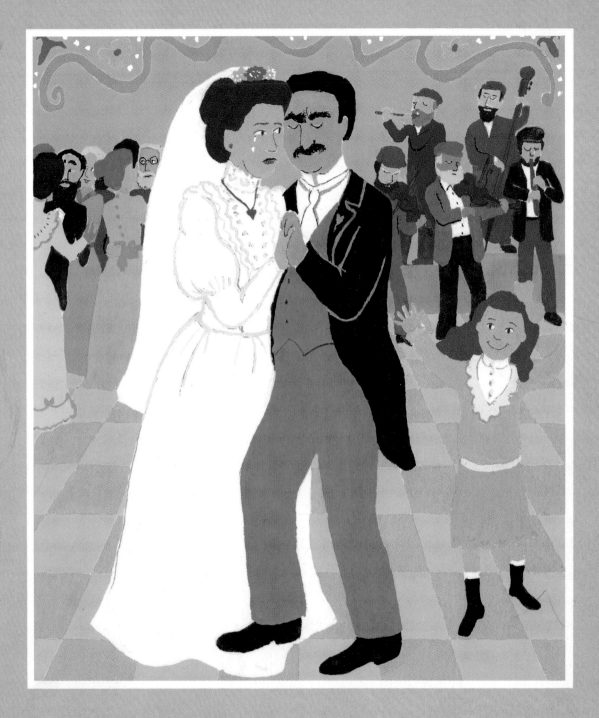

Oma went to her wedding with tears in her eyes.

There was a grand party, and everyone danced.

Oma had to dance with Morris. He was a clumsy oaf.

That night Oma and Morris went to their own house.
Oma told Morris she was going to the bathroom to
change into her nightgown.

Oma knew what she had to do. She climbed out the
bathroom window and ran through the town to her
Tante Sallie's house.

"I've run away from Morris! I can't be his wife. I can't stand to be near him!" Oma cried when her aunt opened the door.

Tante Sallie was kind and loved Oma.
She let her in and comforted her.

The next day the news spread through the town.
Everybody was scandalized.

Oma's parents were so ashamed, they packed her off
to another town far away. Oma lived there with some
cousins for three years until the scandal died down.

When Oma returned to her hometown, people still
whispered behind her back. By then Oma and Morris
were divorced, and Morris was married to someone else.

None of the young men
wanted to court Oma.

Then along came a traveling salesman named Leo.
He was poor, but he was lively and funny and smart.

Oma and Leo fell in love and got married. They had
three daughters. The oldest was my grandmother.

Oma puts her hands down in her lap and stops talking just as I finish the story in my head. She looks at a photograph of Great-grandpa Leo for a long time. Maybe my story really was the same story Oma was telling me. The room is quiet except for Oma's breathing.

Then we hear my mother call, "Celeste, Grandma, it's time for coffee and kuchen!" I help Oma out of her chair. She reaches into her pocket. Every Sunday Oma gives me a surprise. Today it is a shiny silver dollar.

Oma rubs my cheek and kisses me.
We go out to join the rest of the family.